An I Can Read Book®

Adventures of LITTLE BEAR

by

ELSE HOLMELUND MINARIK

pictures by MAURICE SENDAK

BARNES
&NOBLE
BOOKS
NEW YORK

CONTENTS

An I Can Read Book®

LITTLE BEAR

by

ELSE HOLMELUND MINARIK

pictures by MAURICE SENDAK

HarperTrophy®
A Division of HarperCollins*Publishers*

TO BROOKE ELLEN AND WALLY

HarperCollins®, ®, Harper Trophy®, and I Can Read Book®
are trademarks of HarperCollins Publishers Inc.

 Printed in the United States of America. For information address HarperCollins Children's Books, a division of HarperCollins Publishers, 10 East 53rd Street, New York, NY 10022.

Library of Congress Catalog Card Number: 57-9263
ISBN 0-06-024240-X.—ISBN 0-06-024241-8 (lib. bdg.)
ISBN 0-06-444004-4 (pbk.)

CONTENTS

LITTLE BEAR

WHAT WILL LITTLE BEAR WEAR?

It is cold.

See the snow.

See the snow come down.

Little Bear said, "Mother Bear,

I am cold.

See the snow.

I want something to put on."

So Mother Bear made something

for Little Bear.

"See, Little Bear," she said,

"I have something for my little bear.

Here it is.

"Put it on your head."

"Oh," said Little Bear,

"it is a hat.

Hurray! Now I will not be cold."

Little Bear went out to play.

Here is Little Bear.

"Oh," said Mother Bear,

"do you want something?"

"I am cold," said Little Bear.

"I want something to put on."

So Mother Bear made something

for Little Bear.

"See, Little Bear," she said,

"I have something,

something for my little bear.

Put it on."

"Oh," said Little Bear,

"it is a coat.

Hurray! Now I will not be cold."

Little Bear went out to play.

Here is Little Bear again.

"Oh," said Mother Bear,

"do you want something?"

"I am cold," said Little Bear.

"I want something to put on."

So Mother Bear made something
again for Little Bear.
"See, Little Bear," she said,
"here is something,
something for my little bear.
Now you cannot be cold.
Put it on."

"Oh," said Little Bear,
"snow pants. Hurray!
Now I will not be cold."
Little Bear went out to play.

Here is Little Bear again.

"Oh," said Mother Bear,

"what can you want now?"

"I am cold," said Little Bear.

"I want something to put on."

"My little bear," said Mother Bear,

"you have a hat,

you have a coat,

you have snow pants.

Do you want a fur coat, too?"

"Yes," said Little Bear.
"I want a fur coat, too."

Mother Bear took the hat, the coat,
and the snow pants.
"See," said Mother Bear,
"there is the fur coat."

"Hurray!" said Little Bear.
"Here is my fur coat.
Now I will not be cold."

And he was not cold.

What do you think of that?

BIRTHDAY SOUP

"Mother Bear,

Mother Bear,

Where are you?" calls Little Bear.

"Oh, dear, Mother Bear is not here,

and today is my birthday.

"I think my friends will come,
but I do not see a birthday cake.
My goodness—no birthday cake.
What can I do?

The pot is by the fire.
The water in the pot is hot.
If I put something in the water,
I can make Birthday Soup.
All my friends like soup.

Let me see what we have.
We have carrots and potatoes,
peas and tomatoes;
I can make soup with
carrots, potatoes, peas and tomatoes."

So Little Bear begins to make soup

in the big black pot.

First, Hen comes in.

"Happy Birthday, Little Bear," she says.

"Thank you, Hen," says Little Bear.

Ien says, "My! Something smells good here.

; it in the big black pot?"

Yes," says Little Bear,

I am making Birthday Soup.

Vill you stay and have some?"

Oh, yes, thank you," says Hen.

nd she sits down to wait.

Next, Duck comes in.

"Happy Birthday, Little Bear," says Duck.

"My, something smells good.

Is it in the big black pot?"

"Thank you, Duck," says Little Bear.

"Yes, I am making Birthday Soup.

Will you stay and have some with us?"

"Thank you, yes, thank you," says Duck.

And she sits down to wait.

Next, Cat comes in.

"Happy Birthday, Little Bear," he says.

"Thank you, Cat," says Little Bear.

"I hope you like Birthday Soup.

I am making Birthday Soup."

Cat says, "Can you really cook?

If you can really make it,

I will eat it."

"Good," says Little Bear.

"The Birthday Soup is hot,

so we must eat it now.

We cannot wait for Mother Bear.

I do not know where she is.

"Now, here is some soup for you, Hen,"

says Little Bear.

"And here is some soup for you, Duck,

"and here is some soup for you, Cat,

and here is some soup for me.

Now we can all have some Birthday Soup."

Cat sees Mother Bear at the door,

and says, "Wait, Little Bear.

Do not eat yet.

Shut your eyes, and say one, two, three."

Little Bear shuts his eyes
and says, "One, two, three."
Mother Bear comes in with a big cake.
"Now, look," says Cat.

"Oh, Mother Bear," says Little Bear,

"what a big beautiful Birthday Cake!

Birthday Soup is good to eat,

but not as good as Birthday Cake.

I am so happy you did not forget."

"Yes, Happy Birthday, Little Bear!"

says Mother Bear.

"This Birthday Cake is a surprise for you.

I never did forget your birthday,

and I never will."

LITTLE BEAR GOES TO THE MOON

"I have a new space helmet.

I am going to the moon," said Little Bear to

Mother Bear.

"How?" asked Mother Bear.

"I'm going to fly to the moon,"

said Little Bear.

"Fly!" said Mother Bear.

"You can't fly."

"Birds fly," said Little Bear.

"Oh, yes," said Mother Bear.

"Birds fly, but they don't fly to the moon.

And you are not a bird."

"Maybe some birds fly to the moon,

I don't know.

And maybe I can fly like a bird,"

said Little Bear.

"And maybe," said Mother Bear,

"you are a little fat bear cub

with no wings and no feathers.

“Maybe if you jump up

you will come down very fast,

with a big plop.”

“Maybe,” said Little Bear.

“But I’m going now.

Just look for me up in the sky.”

“Be back for lunch,” said Mother.

Little Bear thought.

I will jump from a good high spot,

far up into the sky,

and fly up, up, up.

I will be going too fast

to look at things,

so I will shut my eyes.

Little Bear climbed to the top of a little hill,

and climbed to the top of a little tree,

a very little tree on the little hill,

and shut his eyes and jumped.

Down, down he came with a big plop,

and down the hill he tumbled.

Then he sat up and looked around.

"My, my," he said.

"Here I am on the moon.

"The moon looks just like the earth.

Well, well," said Little Bear.

"The trees here look just like our trees.

The birds look just like our birds.

"And look at this," he said.

"Here is a house that looks just like my hous

I'll go in and see what kind of bears live here

"Look at that," said Little Bear.

"Something to eat is on the table.

It looks like a good lunch for a little bear."

Mother Bear came in and said,

"But who is this?

Are you a bear from Earth?"

"Oh, yes, I am," said Little Bear.

"I climbed a little hill,

and jumped from a little tree,

and flew here, just like the birds."

Well," said Mother Bear.

My little bear did the same thing.

Ie put on his space helmet and flew to Earth.

o I guess you can have his lunch."

Little Bear put his arms around Mother Bea

He said, "Mother Bear, stop fooling.
You are my Mother Bear
and I am your Little Bear,
and we are on Earth, and you know it.
Now may I eat my lunch?"

"Yes," said Mother Bear,
"and then you will have your nap.
For you are my little bear,
and I know it."

LITTLE BEAR'S WISH

"Little Bear," said Mother Bear.

"Yes, Mother," said Little Bear.

"You are not asleep," said Mother Bear.

"No, Mother," said Little Bear.

"I can't sleep."

"Why not?" said Mother Bear.

"I'm wishing," said Little Bear.

"What are you wishing for?"

said Mother Bear.

"I wish that I could sit on a cloud
and fly all around," said Little Bear.
"You can't have that wish, my Little Bear,"
said Mother Bear.

Then I wish that I could find a Viking boat,"
id Little Bear.
And the Vikings would say,
ome along, come along!
ere we go. Away! Away!'"
You can't have that wish, my Little Bear,"
id Mother Bear.

"Then I wish I could find a tunnel,"

said Little Bear.

"Going all the way to China.

I would go to China and come back

with chopsticks for you."

"You can't have that wish, my Little Bear,"

said Mother Bear.

"Then I wish I had a big red car,"

said Little Bear.

"I would go fast, fast.

I would come to a big castle.

"A princess would come out and say,
'Have some cake, Little Bear,'
and I would have some."
"You can't have that wish, my Little Bear,"
said Mother Bear.

"Then I wish," said Little Bear,

"a Mother Bear

would come to me and say,

'Would you like to hear a story?' "

"Well," said Mother Bear,

"maybe you can have that wish.

That is just a little wish."

"Thank you, Mother," said Little Bear.

"That was what I really wanted

all the time."

"What kind of story would you

like to hear?" said Mother Bear.

"Tell me about me,"

said Little Bear.

"Tell me about things

I once did."

"Well," said Mother Bear,

"once you played in the snow,

and you wanted something to put on."

"Oh, yes, that was fun,"

said Little Bear.

"Tell me something more about me."

"Well," said Mother Bear,

"once you put on your space helmet

and played going to the moon."

"That was fun, too,"

said Little Bear.

"Tell me more about me."

"Well," said Mother Bear,

"once you thought you had no Birthday Cake,

so you made Birthday Soup."

"Oh, that was fun," said Little Bear.

"And then you came with the cake.

You always make me happy."

"And now," said Mother Bear,

"you can make me happy, too."

"How?" said Little Bear.

"You can go to sleep,"

said Mother Bear.

"Well, then, I will," said Little Bear.

"Good night, Mother dear."

"Good night, Little Bear.

Sleep well."

The End

FATHER BEAR COMES HOME

An I CAN READ Book®

by ELSE HOLMELUND MINARIK

pictures by MAURICE SENDAK

by the author and artist of LITTLE BEAR

HarperTrophy®
A Division of HarperCollinsPublishers

HarperCollins®, ®, Harper Trophy,® and I Can Read Book®
are trademarks of HarperCollins Publishers Inc.

Library of Congress Catalog Card Number: 59-5794
ISBN 0-06-024230-2
ISBN 0-06-024231-0 (lib. bdg.)
ISBN 0-06-444014-1 (pbk.)

To

URSULA and SUSAN

CONTENTS

LITTLE BEAR AND OWL

"Little Bear," said Mother Bear,

"can you be my fisherman?"

"Yes, I can," said Little Bear.

"Good," said Mother Bear.
"Will you go down
to the river?
Will you catch a fish for us?"

"Yes, I will," said Little Bear.

So Little Bear went down
to the river.
And there he saw Owl.
Owl was sitting on a log.

"Hello, Little Bear," said Owl.
"Hello, Owl," said Little Bear.
"Father Bear is not home.
He is fishing on the ocean.

"But Mother Bear wants a fish now,

so I have to catch one."

"Good," said Owl.

"Catch one."

Little Bear fished.

"I have one," he said.

"Is it too little?"

"It looks good to me," said Owl.

"Well," said Little Bear,

"Father Bear can catch big fish.

He sails in a big boat, too."

Owl said,

“Someday you will be a big bear.

You will catch big fish.

And you will sail in a boat,

like Father Bear.”

“I know what,” said Little Bear.

“We can make believe.

The log can be a boat.

I will be Father Bear.

"You can be you,

and we are fishing."

"Where are we fishing?" asked Owl.

"On the ocean," said Little Bear.

"All right," said Owl.

"Hurray!" said Little Bear.
"See what I have."

"What is it?" asked Owl.

"An octopus," said Little Bear.

"Oh," said Owl.
"But see what I have."

"What is it?" asked Little Bear.

"A whale," said Owl.

"But a whale is too big,"
said Little Bear.

"This is a little whale," said Owl.

Just then Mother Bear came along.

"Where is the fish?" she asked.

Little Bear laughed. He said,
"How about an octopus?"
"An octopus!" said Mother Bear.

"Well, then," said Owl,

"how about a little whale?"

"A WHALE!!" said Mother Bear.

"No, thank you. No whale."

"Then how about this fish?"

said Little Bear.

"Yes, thank you," said Mother Bear,
"that is just what I want."

Little Bear said,
"You will see.
When I am as big as Father Bear,
I will catch a real octopus."

"Yes, and sail in a real boat,"
said Owl.

"I know it," said Mother Bear.

Owl said,
"Little Bear fishes very well."

"Oh, yes," said Mother Bear,
"he fishes very well, indeed.

"He is a real fisherman,

just like his father."

FATHER BEAR COMES HOME

"Hello, Hen."

"Hello, Little Bear."

"Guess what!" said Little Bear.

"What?"

"Father Bear is coming home today."

"Is he?" said Hen.

"Where was he?"

"Fishing," said Little Bear,

"out on the ocean.

Far out on the ocean."

"My!" said Hen.

"Out on the ocean. Well!"

"Yes," said Little Bear,

"and what if he saw a mermaid?"

"A mermaid!" said Hen.

"Yes, a little mermaid," said Little Bear.
"And maybe she could come home with him."

"Ooh!" said Hen.
"A mermaid at your house.

"I want to see her.

I am coming home with you."

They walked along,

and there was Duck.

"Hello, Duck," said Little Bear.

"Father Bear is coming home today.

Guess where he was."

"Where?" asked Duck.

"Fishing," said Little Bear,
"far out on the ocean.
Out where the mermaids are, maybe."

"Yes," said Hen,
"and we are going to see one."

"What is a mermaid like?"
asked Duck.

"A mermaid!" said Little Bear.
"Why, a mermaid is very pretty.
A mermaid's hair is blue and green.
Like the ocean,
blue and green."

"She is coming home with Father Bear,"

said Hen.

"Ooh!" said Duck.

"I want to see her, too.

I am coming home with you."

They walked along,
and there was Cat.

"Hello, Cat," said Little Bear.
"Father Bear is coming home today.
He was fishing on the ocean,
far out on the ocean."

"Yes," said Hen,

"out where the mermaids are."

"And," said Duck,

"we are going to see one."

"Where are you going to see one?"

asked Cat.

"One is coming home with Father Bear,"
said Hen.

"Yes," said Duck,
"and her hair is blue and green."

"And maybe her eyes are silver,"

said Little Bear,

"silver, like the moon."

"Silver eyes!" said Cat.

"How pretty!

I will have to see her.

I am coming home with you."

They walked along,
and there was Little Bear's house.
And there was Father Bear.
He had come home.

Little Bear ran to Father Bear
and hugged him.
Father Bear hugged Little Bear.

Then Father Bear said hello
to Hen, and Duck, and Cat.

"We came to see the mermaid,"
said Hen.

"Her hair is blue and green,"
said Duck.

"Her eyes are silver like the moon,"
said Cat.

"And she is very pretty," said Hen.

"How nice!" said Father Bear.

"Where is she?"

"You have her,"

said Hen and Duck and Cat.

"Oh?" said Father Bear.

He looked at Little Bear.

"No mermaid?" asked Little Bear.

"No little mermaid?"

"No," said Father Bear,

"no little mermaid."

"Well!" said Hen.

"My!" said Duck.

"Really!" said Cat.

They all looked at Little Bear.

"But I said maybe," said Little Bear,

"I did say maybe."

"Come, now," said Father Bear.

"See what I have for all of you.

Sea shells.

You can hear the ocean in them.

And maybe you can hear the mermaids, too.

Maybe."

HICCUPS

Little Bear was happy.

Father Bear was home.

He was in his chair reading.

Cat, Duck, Hen and Little Bear
were playing with the sea shells.
They were trying to hear the ocean.

"I hear it," said Cat.
"So do I," said Duck.
"I do, too," said Hen.
"I do, hic—too," said Little Bear.
"Hic!" he said again.

"You have the hiccups," said Cat.

"Have some water, Little Bear,"
said Mother Bear.

So Little Bear had some water,
but he did not stop hiccuping.

“Hello, everyone!”

Owl was at the door.

“Hello, Owl,” said Mother Bear,

“you are the very one for us.

You are always so wise.

Water will not stop Little Bear’s hiccups.

What can we do?”

"Well, now," said Owl,
"water is very good,
but he must hold his breath, too."

"Hic," said Little Bear.
"Hic, how can I—hic—
hold my—hic—breath, too?
Hic?"

"You can," said Owl.

"Try."

Little Bear did as Owl said.

"See?" said Little Bear.

"No more hic—hic—hiccups."

He was hiccuping again.

"This always works," said Cat.

And he gave Little Bear

a slap on the back.

"Oof!" said Little Bear. "Hic!

That's not—hic—any good."

"Someone is by the door,"
said Cat.
"Someone is coming in."

Little Bear laughed.
"Look at—hic—that," he said.
"It's—hic—only Duck and Hen."

"Did we make the hiccups go away?"

asked Duck.

"No—hic—you did not,"

said Little Bear.

Father Bear roared—

"There is too much noise here.

Who is making all that noise?"

He looked at Owl, Cat, Hen and Duck.

"How can I read with all that noise?"

he asked.

And he looked at Little Bear.

"Noise?" said Little Bear.

"I was only hiccuping."

"What was that?" said Father Bear.

"Hiccuping," said Little Bear.
"I was only hiccuping."

Father Bear laughed.
"Hiccuping!" he said.

"I can't hear any hiccups."

"But I was hiccuping," said Little Bear.

"All right," said Father Bear,
"hiccup for me."

But Little Bear could not do it.

“Come, now,” said Father Bear.

“One, two, three, hiccup.”

No, Little Bear could not do it.

“Well, well,” said Father Bear.

“I guess he can’t hiccup any more.”

"Why should he?" said Mother Bear.

"Who wants hiccups anyway?" said Hen.

"That's right," said Cat and Duck.

"Who wants hiccups?"

Owl said,

"You can still stop them my way.

Little Bear didn't really try."

They all laughed,

and Owl laughed, too.

"You just have to know how to do it,"

said Owl.

"That's right," said Father Bear.

"You just have to know how to do it."

"We can picnic here," said Mother Bear.

"It is nice here, by the river."

"Let's go for a swim," said Father Bear.

Owl said,

"Little Bear swims like a fish."

"Yes," said Little Bear,

"but mermaids swim best of all.

I still wish we had a mermaid.

Maybe there is a mermaid in the river."

"I never saw one," said Cat.

"Well," said Little Bear,
"she may be shy.
She may not want us to see her.
If we could make believe we are asleep,
she might come and look at us."

“Would she like us?” asked Hen.

“Of course,” said Little Bear.

“She might want to play with you,”
said Mother Bear.

"Then I would jump up
and play with her," said Little Bear.

"Oh," said Owl,
"but if she is shy,
she might jump back in the river.
Then all we could see
would be bubbles."

"I see some bubbles now,"

said Little Bear.

"And where there are bubbles,

there may be a mermaid.

I'm going in."

“If you find a mermaid,”

said Father Bear,

“ask her to picnic with us.”

“Yes, do that,” said Mother Bear.

“Ask her.”

"I will," said Little Bear,

"because you never can tell.

She might really come back with me."

"Yes indeed," said Father Bear,

"she might really come back with you.

Because you never can tell

about mermaids.

You never can tell."

A KISS FOR LITTLE BEAR

An I CAN READ Book®

by ELSE HOLMELUND MINARIK

Pictures by MAURICE SENDAK

HarperTrophy®
A Division of HarperCollins*Publishers*

A KISS FOR LITTLE BEAR

Library of Congress Catalog Card Number: 68-16820
ISBN 0-06-024298-1. — ISBN 0-06-024299-X (lib. bdg.)
ISBN 0-06-444050-8 (pbk.)

A Kiss for Little Bear

"This picture makes me happy,"

said Little Bear.

“Hello, Hen.

This picture is for Grandmother.

Will you take it to her, Hen?"

"Yes, I will," said Hen.

Grandmother was happy.

"This kiss is for Little Bear," she said.

"Will you take it to him, Hen?"

"I will be glad to," said Hen.

Then Hen saw some friends.

She stopped to chat.

“Hello, Frog.

I have a kiss for Little Bear.

It is from his grandmother.

Will you take it to him, Frog?"

"OK," said Frog.

But Frog saw a pond.

He stopped to swim.

"Hi, Cat.

I have a kiss for Little Bear.

It is from his grandmother.

Take it to him, will you?

Cat—hi!

Here I am, in the pond.

Come and get the kiss."

"Oogh!" said Cat.

But he came and got the kiss.

Cat saw a nice spot to sleep.

"Little Skunk,

I have a kiss for Little Bear.

It is from his grandmother.

Take it to him like a good little skunk."

Little Skunk was glad to do that.

But then he saw another little skunk.

She was very pretty.

He gave the kiss to her.

And she gave it back.

And he gave it back.

And then Hen came along.

"Too much kissing," she said.

"But this is Little Bear's kiss,
from his grandmother,"
said Little Skunk.

"Indeed!" said Hen.

"Who has it now?"

Little Skunk had it.

Hen got it back.

She ran to Little Bear,

and she gave him the kiss.

"It is from your grandmother,"

she said.

"It is for the picture you sent her."

"Take one back to her,"

said Little Bear.

"No," said Hen.

"It gets all mixed up!"

The skunks decided to get married.

They had a lovely wedding.

Everyone came.

And Little Bear was best man.